Harrison Berry

Slavery and Abolitionism

As viewed by a Georgia slave

Harrison Berry

Slavery and Abolitionism
As viewed by a Georgia slave

ISBN/EAN: 9783337410339

Printed in Europe, USA, Canada, Australia, Japan

Cover: Foto ©Andreas Hilbeck / pixelio.de

More available books at **www.hansebooks.com**

3

SLAVERY

AND

ABOLITIONISM,

AS VIEWED BY A

GEORGIA SLAVE.

BY HARRISON BERRY,
THE PROPERTY OF S. W. PRICE, COVINGTON, GEORGIA.

ATLANTA, GEORGIA :
M. LYNCH & CO., PUBLISHERS.
PRINTED AT THE CRUSADER OFFICE.
1861.

PREFACE

I could not hope for the acquiescence of my Southern masters in this my views on Mr. Lincoln's Inaugural, were it not from the fact, that his party is a mixed up affair of colored and white, all equally bent and determined to carry out their views, regardless of the affecting consequences whatever; and when we read the speech of a colored man by the name of Charles L. Redmond, delivered in Boston at an Anti-slavery Convention, held in May, 1856, when we hear him say, "remembering Washington as a Slaveholder, he (Redmond) could spit upon him;" and when we hear him applauded, in the highest degree of mirth, by his factional party, while the conservative men groan under the sound of that blasphemous language, may be an excuse for one poor Slave whom that party pretends to be helping, (but is actually doing him harm;) and when my Southern masters take into consideration the many tricks fixed up to deceive the poor Europeans, who are constantly immigrating to their States, by telling them that if they vote for the pro-slavery candidate, it will be the means of enslaving them, I am in hopes will be a pleader for their sympathies with this my presumption.

The Anarchy predicted by my first edition, written some eight months before the election, stating that the election of a sectional man to the Presidency would inevitably bring about the state of things which stands before us in a monstrous form at the present time, may be conceded to me as a good guesser, at least. Under these considerations, together with others stated in the commentary, I hope they will forgive me for making the attack, and extend to me that sympathy I do so earnestly desire.

HARRISON BERRY.

CERTIFICATES.

From Hon. L. J. Gartrell.

From evidences in my possession of the most reliable character, I am satisfied that the Slave, Harrison Berry, is the author of a pamphlet, entitled "Slavery and Abolitionism, as viewed by a Georgia Slave." I know him personally, have conversed with him, and believe him capable of writing it.

LUCIUS J. GARTRELL,
Late member of Congress, 4th District.

Atlanta, April 14, 1861.

From W. W. Clark, Esqr.

I am the owner of the wife of Harrison Berry—have had him hired for two years—have seen and read his manuscript—and can certify to the fact that he is the author of a pamphlet entitled "Slavery and Abolitionism, as viewed by a Georgia Slave." He is a "Southern Rights" negro—a good and honest servant, and his book is worthy of public consideration and patronage.

W. W. CLARK,

Covington, April 10, 1861.   Attorney at Law, Covington, Ga.

From A. G. Ware, Esqr.

I have had ample opportunity to know, and am satisfied beyond doubt, that Harrison Berry is the author of a pamphlet entitled "Slavery and Abolitionism, as viewed by a Georgia Slave." I saw the original manuscript, and have read the printed work—they are identical. I have known Harrison for several years, and know him to be competent to write such a work.   A. G. WARE,

Agent Macon & Western Railroad, Atlanta, Ga.

From Rev. Lewis Lawshe.

I have known Harrison Berry since 1842. I knew his old master, the late David Berry, and all of the family. Harrison has all the time been a good servant. It has always been his highest ambition to do his duty at anything his master set him at. Harrison is a sensible boy, and pretty well educated, and is, without a doubt, the *bona fide* author of the pamphlet entitled "Slavery and Abolitionism, as viewed by a Georgia Slave." He has expressed the same sentiments to me in conversation, that are set forth in his book, saying that he would let Fred Douglass, and other Abolitionists, know that the slaves of the South were not fools enough to believe that they were benefitting them, or even intended to *try to benefit them.* There is not a shadow of a doubt, in my mind, but what Harrison Berry did write the above named book, as I have had sufficient opportunity to know the fact, having been acquainted with him for the last nineteen years.

It would be well for every Planter to obtain a copy of his work, and read it to his slaves.   LEWIS LAWSHE.

Atlanta, Georgia, April 18th, 1861.

From the Banner & Baptist.

"ABOLITION AND SLAVERY," BY A SLAVE.—This pamphlet is now going on its mission. Many, no doubt, would be pleased to see it, besides those who have sent their orders. The work bears ample evidence of having been written entirely by the professed author. No one will suppose that a negro, with but limited education, could write anything like a model work on such a subject. But Harrison Berry has done well, and his book ought to be, and will be read. We think no farmer would be the loser to read it to his negroes.

From the Journal of Commerce, Jr.

THE TESTIMONY OF A SLAVE.—We have received from Atlanta, Georgia, a pamphlet entitled "Slavery and Abolitionism," written by a negro who subscribes himself "Harrison Berry, the property of S. W. Price, Covington, Georgia." This man is a full blooded African, forty-five years of age, and learned to read and write while employed as an errand boy in a law office. He has since been a hard student, and has acquired a fair amount of information. This pamphlet is published by himself, and copy-righted for his benefit exclusively. He says in the preface: "I am a slave, and have been all my life, and therefore claim the opportunity, at least, of knowing what Slavery is, and what it is not." He was induced to write upon the subject of Slavery from a firm conviction that Abolitionist agitators are the worst enemies of the slave.

There could be no more befitting rebuke to the Abolition meddlers, than is conveyed in the words which come from this oppressed subject of their sympathy, who is "a slave," and "knows what slavery is." Moreover, the simple facts noted above, are evidence sufficient to refute the assertion that the slave is a down-trodden creature, kept in ignorance, and debarred from all privileges. But it seems he is able to speak for himself.

From the Griffin Union.

HARRISON BERRY.—We have just finished reading a pamphlet from the pen of this personage. We know Harrison, and know him to be a Slave, and a black one at that; and although the matter of his pamphlet is not arranged with that perspicuity and system that would mark an accomplished writer, there are truths told by Harrison that it would be well for many white men, and all black ones, to ponder and profit by. That Slavery is the proper status for the black man, no one can doubt, who will properly investigate the subject. In his native wilds he is a savage, with no hope of improvement. A free man among white people, he is inferior, and cannot rise to a level with his neighbors, and has all his work to do when in health, under disadvantages that few can overcome; and, when sick, he has no one to care for him; whilst the Slave has only his work to do when in health with all the advantages his masters position and superior management can afford him, and, when sick, his master is bound by law and interest to provide for his necessities. And it is true, as Harrison says, that the Abolitionists are his worst enemies, inasmuch as all their efforts only tend to draw the cords of servitude more tightly around him, and deprive him of many indulgencies that he would otherwise enjoy.

INTRODUCTION.

HARRISON BERRY, the author of these pages, was born in Jones county, Georgia, November, 1816, and is now a little more than forty-four years old. He was born a Slave, and became the property of Mr. David Berry, but was given to his daughter as a part of her marriage portion. This daughter married Mr. S. W. Price, who, in turn, became the owner of Harrison, and so remains at the present time. Harrison removed, with his old master, David Berry, to Butts county, Georgia, when about ten years old, and was placed in the Law Office of John V. Berry, a son of the former. His business was to wait upon his young master, run on errands, go to the Post Office, and to perform other like service. These employments were such as to leave a good deal of time at his own disposal, which he was induced to improve in learning to read and write.

When he became older and stronger, he was put to work on the farm, but continued to improve his mind by reading such books as were furnished him by the younger members of the Berry family; so that by the time he had grown to man's estate, he had made considerable proficiency in History, and had picked up a fair share of general information.

At the present time he is engaged in the business of Boot-making. He was induced to write upon the subject of Slavery from a firm conviction that Abolitionist agitators are the worst enemies of the Slave, and from the settled opinion that Slavery is according to the Divine Law. He believes, furthermore, that Southern Slaves are in a much better condition than if they had remained in their native land, and this opinion has been formed after a fair and impartial examination of the subject in the light of history, philosophy and religion. While the work has imperfections, (and what human work has not?) still the reader will find much to interest him in these pages, and I would bespeak for the author a favorable reception of his little offering to the cause of Truth and Justice.   H. C. HORNADY.

ATLANTA, GEORGIA, February 26, 1860.

PREFACE.

In offering this address to the public, I do it with the most profound humility, knowing it to be a task worthy of a better learned and more intelligent writer than myself. But when it is taken into consideration, the cause by which I was actuated may be an excuse for my presumption; for I am a Slave, and have been all my life, and, therefore, claim the opportunity, at least, of knowing what Slavery is, and what it is not. And in showing the effect the agitation of Slavery has upon the Slaves generally, I have endeavored to keep within the boundaries of moderation, unless forced by undoubted facts to depart therefrom. In speaking of the citizens of the Northern States, I have, in a great many places, summed them all up together; but my intention is to cast no reflections, whatever, upon the conservative citizens of that section. My address is to the fanatical Abolitionists, who call themselves Republicans. To them, and them alone, have I written.

Written by   HARRISON BERRY,
The property of S. W. Price, residing in Butts county, Georgia.

TO THE PUBLIC.

Covington, July 7, 1860.

Harrison:—I have been so busily engaged that I could not reply to your first letter. By this letter I give you full permission to print and publish your MS. I presume that this statement will be sufficient, as I give you permission to use this letter as may best suit your desire. I wish you success.

S. W. PRICE.

Harrison is the property of Mr. Price, of Butts county, Georgia; is a Shoemaker by trade, and has been steadily employed at his trade for many years. In the latter part of 1853 he was employed by F. M. Eddleman & Bro., Shoe dealers in this city, and remained in their employ for several years afterwards, with some intermission. As I was one of that firm, and actively engaged in the business, I had every opportunity to become acquainted with his sentiments, and to judge of his ability to express himself upon paper. I am not aware when and where he learned to write, but when he came into our employ he could write legibly. This pamphlet was written under most unfavorable circumstances, and is, as I know, the result of much labor on his part. His daily service was performed in the Shoe-shop, and his nights, and I might add Sundays, were devoted to reading and writing. The original manuscript was written, for the most part, in the shop, and as conveniences for writing are not usually provided in such places, the *lap-board* was converted into, or, at least, made to serve the purpose of a table. I frequently found his manuscript in the shop, and would sometimes read it, as a matter of amusement. As I saw it in this way, it was, to me, quite an unconnected affair. Nevertheless, in its chaotic state, the ideas intended to be conveyed were often forcibly and truthfully set forth. I was not aware, until 1857, that he had any notion of collecting this matter together in the form of a pamphlet, and, while I did not doubt his ability to do so, still I did not, at that time, suppose he would do so. In the latter part of 1857, however, he informed me that he had prepared and arranged the manuscript, and desired that I should read it. I did so hurriedly, and returned it, advising him to get others to examine it.

The original manuscript was, however, afterwards sent to Col. Logan, of Griffin, for his inspection, and while in his possession was destroyed by fire.

In 1860, Harrison applied to me again to examine his production, which he had re-written, and made some additions. I read it carefully, and wrote him that there were some errors of *fact* in it that should be corrected before it went to press. He afterwards informed me that he had gone over it and had made the corrections to which he supposed I alluded, and thus it went to the press.

I will not merely say that I *think* he wrote it, for I can safely say that I know him to be the author—the sentiments are his for I have heard him express them time and again, long before I ever dreamed of his writing a book.

Harrison fully understands the position of a *Slave*, and has uniformly kept himself in his proper place. He is neither insolent or impudent, but humble and polite. He is honest and trustworthy, and has ever enjoyed the confidence of those who know him. His complexion is fully up to the African standard, not having, I suppose, a particle of white blood in his veins. He says he was, when a boy, the blackest, ugliest little negro in the region, and was frequently annoyed by travelers stopping, as they were passing the road, to comment upon his extreme color. He has been, and is yet, a hard student; has read a great deal, and his reading has been varied.

While in the employ of my brother and myself he read *Josephus*, and compared it minutely with Sacred History. He reads for information, and not for amusement, and always put forth his greatest effort to understand his subject.

His hate for an Abolitionist is supreme, and when expressing his contempt for them, generally exhausts the vocabulary of adjectives at his command. At first I thought this strange, and had my doubts as to his sincerity. But now I have no doubt on that point. I have heard him give his reasons frequently, and consider them forcible and good. He has remarked to me often, when applying for a pass, that the privileges of Slaves had been curtailed on account of the foolish interference of Abolitionists. He thinks that but for this interference of Abolitionists, Slaves would be allowed all the privileges they are capable of enjoying. He thinks Slavery is the proper condition for the negro, resulting in more happiness than nominal freedom. He has often remarked in my ·hearing, that there was no such a thing as a free negro in this country, (meaning the whole country.)

His pamphlet is published by himself, copy-righted for his benefit, and the profits from its sale, should any arise, will be his. I cheerfully commend it to the public, believing that it should be liberally patronized. The time he has devoted to writing his book, is generally occupied by other Slaves in making their pocket change.

A. M. EDDLEMAN.

ATLANTA, GEORGIA, February 26, 1861.

SLAVERY AND ABOLITIONISM.

HAVING, for several years, viewed the agitation of the question of Slavery to be an evil dangerous and highly detrimental to the common good, and particularly that of the South, I was moved, in 1857, to write an address to the Abolition party, showing, as plainly as I could, the inconsistency of their proceedings. I gave it to the editor of the "Empire State," at Griffin, after it had been examined by gentlemen of Atlanta, Covington and Newnan; but its being consumed in the late conflagration in Griffin, necessitates me to write another. Seeing my views forcibly exemplified in the late treason at Harper's Ferry may be a guarantee to me, granted by all conservative men, the privilege of addressing them again. This privilege might be more readily admitted, when you take into consideration that I am one of those whom the Abolitionists pretend to be helping.

I will now examine what this monster is—this seven-headed, ten-horned beast. It seems to be one of considerable power, for it now threatens the dissolution of a Union formed by men who are not paralleled by any that have graced the annals of history. Well, then, if this Union was so dearly obtained, it then follows that its citizens ought, of all things, to love and cherish it. And one who does not do it, is unfaithful to his country; but one who seeks to disturb its peace, while it is endeavoring to deal, with an impartial hand, to each constituent, the portion designed him by the Constitution, is a traitor of the deepest dye.

Yet, we find men doing it. And for what? For nothing but because the people of one section of the country wish to engage in a branch of business which would not be profitable to those of the other, notwithstanding it is as lawful a branch of business as that of manufacturing—the Constitution granting them, each, the same protection. Nevertheless, they claim it to be unlawful; and when it is shown to be both Constitutional and lawful, they then, being left no other alternative, flee from that to the Higher Law —which I intend to discuss in its proper place.

Kind reader, I expect, by this time, you would like to hear what that question is. I answer, SLAVERY. Well, let us see what Slavery is. An eminent writer says: "A Slave, in the ordinary sense of the term, is an individual at the absolute disposal of another, who has a right to employ him and treat him as he pleases." But let us see what he says after this. Hear him: "But the state of Slavery is susceptible of numerous modifications; and it has been usual, in most countries where it has been long established, to limit, in various ways, the power of the master over the Slave." You see, this eminent writer talks like a book.

Kind reader, I now beg you to bear with me a little, while I discuss, in a very abridged manner, the origin of Slavery. It seems that an authentic account of the origin of Slavery is hard to get hold of. The best to be found is only probable; and I think the most probable conjecture is, that it grew out of a state of war. The captives taken in war, in ancient times, seem to have belonged to the victors; and these they had the exclusive right to treat as they pleased. And it was the custom of the Africans to put to death all that could not be advantageously enslaved, centuries before it existed in any part of Europe or America. It is not only in Africa we find Slavery existing centuries ago, but in the midst of the chosen people of God; for it was the law in Judea for the parents to sell their children. So it was in Rome. And it did not stop at that; for if a citizen got in debt over what he was able to pay, he was taken and sold for the same. So we see Slavery existing thousands of years ago.

But let us see where and when it commenced with us. We find that in 1442, the Portuguese commenced the traffic. It was, however, of trifling extent, until the sixteenth century, when, in consequence of the rapid destruction of the Indians employed in the mines of St. Domingo or Hayti, that Charles V. authorized, in 1517, the introduction into the island of African Slaves, from the establishment of the Portuguese on the coast of Guinea. The importation of Africans once begun, it rapidly spread itself over Europe and America. Sir John Hawkins was the first Englishman who engaged in it; and such was the ardor of our countrymen engaged in it, that they exported, from Africa, over 300,000 Slaves between the years 1680 and 1700; and, between 1700 and 1786, 610,000 Africans were imported into Jamaica; and, adding those imported into other continental colonies, and those shipped to the other Islands, the quantity must have been immense.

The same writer says: "But those who inquire dispassionately into the subject, will come to the conclusion, that, instead of being injured, the Slaves have gained by being carried from the New to the Old World."

Let us see what he says next. He says: "Speaking generally, the Negroes are in the lowest state of abandonment, possessing merely the rudiments of the most indispensable arts—a prey to the vilest superstition and tyranny, without any tincture of learning, and with little or no regard for the future. The circumstances under which they are placed in their native land may, perhaps account for the low state in which we find them. But, however explained, the genuine Negroes of Africa are admitted, even by those least inclined to depreciate them, to be, for the most part, either ferocious savages, or stupid, sensual and indolent."

So, we see what he says; but I shall not stop to comment on that now, but will notice it in its proper place.

Kind reader, I will now jump over the years from 1786 to 1794, and see what Congress thought of Slavery at that time.

By the Act of March 22, 1794, the Slave Trade was prohibited. The Act of May 10, 1800, applied to foreigners residing in the United States, and forbid citizens being engaged in foreign ships in the Slave Trade. By the Act of March 2, 1807, vessels with Slaves on board were to be forfeited—the naval forces to be employed to enforce the Act. By the Act of April 20, 1818, the importation of Negroes, or persons of color, to be held to service or labor, was prohibited. By Act of March 3, 1819, the naval ships would send to the United States, for confiscation, any ships detected in the Slave Trade; and a bounty was offered, of $25, for each Negro captured and delivered to the United States Marshal. By Act of May 15, 1820, the Slave Trade was declared to be piracy; and any citizen detected in the Trade should suffer death. By the Act of September 20, 1850, the Slave Trade in the District of Columbia was prohibited; no Slaves to be brought into the District for sale as merchandize, and all Slave depots to be broken up.

Now, it does look to me like Congress was working at the abolition of Slavery the right way, and the only way it can ever be accomplished. For Slavery might be abolished in the States for awhile, but if it were not stopped at its source, it would only break through with tenfold velocity. It would inevitably diffuse itself throughout the world in such a manner that it would be next to impossible to ever stop its progress, or mitigate its effects. But these Northern agitators of Slavery were not satisfied with the proceedings of Congress on the subject. They, I suppose, intended to abolish it in the States first, and then march their forces to the Atlantic, and embark them on board of canoes, and take the vessels on the high seas engaged in the Slave Trade, and bring them to taw, too! These would-be-called philanthropists seemed to have forgotten the old maxim that, "if you wish to find the spring, go to the head of the branch;" for they could stop the *boil*, and then the strength of the current would be greatly mitigated. But their discrimination seems to be quite limited. Had it not been, they could have seen, long ago, that the agitation of Slavery put a manacle on the hands of every Slave south of Mason and Dixon's Line. But I don't think they cared for that. The Sacred Scriptures, by which they pretend to be governed, would have taught them, at a mere glimpse, that to preserve peace in a country, even at a sacrifice, was the best mode of sustaining their country.

I will simply point out a few passages of the Scripture, by observation, and not by the letter, as they will be perfectly understood by ten-year old boys, familiar with the Bible. It is well known that the New Testament teaches peace—peace—peace—prosperity and happiness, from the first of Matthew to the end of Revelations ; and that, too, in one uninterrupted chain of admonition. We see Slavery in Judea long before the coming of Christ, for we see it in Abraham's days. He had some three hundred born in his own house; and, certainly, if they were born in his own house, they must have been his. And if it had been a sin in the sight of God and His angels, Abraham, being a righteous man, conversing with and entertaining angels directly from Heaven, would, it is very likely, have been very severely rebuked for having those illegal servants, and requiring them to wait on and serve the angels, while they dined in his house. But this is but one of hundreds of instances of the like character. But, coming down to the Christian era, we find it more fully developed ; for it was not an angel, but God Himself saw it, was among it, tolerated it, and supported it, in, and by, the teachings of His sublime Gospel. For He was willing for Cæsar to have his, and God His. We see, then, that Christ did not hesitate a moment to cause to be restored to its rightful owner the penny with the image of Cæsar, that Pagan usurper, that idol-worshiper, who would compel whole nations to adore his wicked and polluted idols. This wicked monarch's image we see thus acknowledged by Christ Himself; to be honored, rather than disturb the peace of the people. And how much more ought it to be the duty of a wicked and rebellious set of Abolitionists to render unto the South her rights? We see the Apostles teaching peace all through the New Testament. We see, in the Epistles, they exhort Servants to be obedient to their masters; and not only in words do we find this, but in all their practice. For, on one occasion, when a Slave had run away from his master, and went to Paul, he does not hesitate a moment, but sends him back to his lawful owner. This shows that Christ and the Apostles had quite a different view of Slavery to that of our modern factionists of the United States.

I might enlarge on this question in this place, had I time and space; but, as I shall have to recur to the Sacred Writings again, in the course of this address, I will leave it for the present.

We will now examine some of the leading principles of the Abolition party It is not that I am opposed to freedom, that actuates me to address them in the manner which I do, for I believe it to be one of the greatest blessings earthly, when not contaminated with fanatical dispositions. But rather would I die, were I a citizen of the United States, than to disturb the peace, or act in any way that would be detrimental to the onward progress and prosperity of my country. For, of all the Governments that now exist, or have ever existed, this perhaps is the least contaminated with injustice—the Constitution granting to every native born, or adopted citizen, the freedom of speech, and the power, at the ballot-box, of making their own laws to be governed by. What a lesson it ought to be to the American citizen, to view four-fifths of Europe and Asia having no more power to make the laws by which they are governed than the Slaves of this country who are not citizens! I sometimes think that a man living in, and enjoying, the many advantages this country has over others, and who would act with a party that is endeavoring to frustrate the conservative ones, ought to be denounced as a traitor, and excluded from all public trust, from the simple fact that he would prostitute all the power guaranteed to him in his office; and consequently, is no longer worthy of public confidence. In this land of Republican freedom, such a character is, of all citizens, the most dangerous. The management of the Government being in the hands of the people, it is emphatically their duty to brand with infamy any person, or persons, who would presume to rebel against the great Constitutional compact; that others might know the consequences of entering into a like rebellion. But, yet, we have some such, standing in the first positions within the gift of the people. And how do they get there? I answer, by deceiving and gulling the great masses of the people; that is how they get there. Let every man give to his children the best education he can afford, and the natural capacity of the child is capable of receiving; and let the parents instil into their bosoms the importance of the Union of the States, and the preservation of peace and harmony. Thus educated and instructed, while a child, it would be as hard to erase it from his heart as to mar the natural form of his body; and, in a few years you would have a majority that could, and would, defy all the fanaticism that could be engendered by the whole combined Abolition faction. We have no cause to complain of the hard tried Editors of true patriotism. God knows they have had every thing to contend with. It matters not how wide may be the views of conservative Editors on questions of internal improvement, taxes, tariffs, or any other question of policy. Whenever the rights guaranteed to them by the true patriots of '76 is encroached upon, they present one solid phalanx, and drive back the opposers of their liberties. These are they who stand on watch, as sentinels, for the main army of occupation. These are the ones who sit on the towers on the walls, and when they see danger, cry with a loud voice, "To arms, to arms!" But what must I say about the fanatical Editors? Can I say they are not designedly deceiving their followers? Don't they know that the old hobby horse is down long ago? Don't they know that the one they now have in the field is the same old horse, and that everybody knows the old fellow's make, notwithstanding they have rubbed vitriol all over him, and have changed his color? You had just as well turn the old fellow out to grass, for he's broken down—he never had any bottom at first. But, say you, we have never had a fair chance, from the fact that we never had a rider until the last race.

Kind reader, I must now stop nonsense, and proceed to facts. In the first place, I should like to know for what purpose the Abolitionists oppose Slavery? Secondly, I should like to know what advantage it is, or can be, to them? If they don't wish to speculate in some way or other, why are they so sensitive on the subject of Slavery? The agitation excludes them entirely from a religious design, as I have shown above. For, without that peaceful and philanthropical principle taught by Christ and His Apostles, no genuine religion can exist. It would be better for them, if they are acting on religious principles, to suffer wrong for the preservation of peace, than to exact their rights at the expense of disturbances. This is plainly proven by Holy Writ, when it says, "Blessed is the peacemaker." Well, then, tell me what business have you with Slavery? It is known, by all sensible men, that it existed before the formation of the Constitution of the United States Government; and if it was tolerated then, it must, without a change in that instrument, be so now. You call yourselves Republicans; and if you are, in the strict sense of the word, you are compelled to abide by its teachings; and if governed by its teachings, you must necessarily be governed by the teachings of the Supreme Court. Its decisions are the *laws* of the land. It cannot be said that you are so ignorant as to believe that you are benefitting the Slaves, for you are an educated class of gentlemen, who take the Southern papers, and are thereby enabled to see and read for yourselves, that the Slaves are much worse treated when that question is agitated. My dear sirs, upon you and your heads will cry more blood than any planter, or planters, of the South; for when the masters and Slaves are getting on just as well as they wish to, you commence your infernal agitations. The master goes to town, he gets his paper, he reads that the Abolition party is making a great to-do about freeing the Slaves; he becomes sullen, contrary and ill; he goes to the field, and if the least thing is wrong, he is in the right humor for a fuss; he accuses the Slave of idleness; the Slave commences quarreling, the master makes at him; the Slave perhaps runs away; he is caught, and then made to feel the anger of a master goaded to madness by the officious intermeddling and hypocritical sympathy of a people who neither understand, nor wish to understand, his true position or his interest. And for what? Simply because the Abolitionist is endeavoring to take the property of a half century's hard labor, and leave the poor old man without a Slave, who had invested the last cent he had in Slaves; and now the Abolitionists are endeavoring to take them from him, and leave him penniless. Now, to say that this is a general thing, I have no intention of doing; but that such a state of things has happened, under my observation, is without a doubt. And, as I have said above, speaking of Congress legislating on the Slave Trade, if you intend to find the spring, go to the head of the branch. Now, if our masters were

allowed to enjoy the property acquired by the toils of so many
years, in peace and safety, what do you suppose would be the relation between master and Slave? I need not add, that the use
(disconnected with the abuse) of Slavery is not a sin. So your
fanatical factions, causing the abuse, become the primary oppress-.
ors of the Slaves. Yes, indeed, you are absolutely the worst enemy the Slave has ever had to encounter with yet, and, I hope, ever
may have. But the present state of things is nothing to what it
would be, if you were permitted to carry out your pernicious
proceedings, now being organized under the name of Republican-
ism. But I will recur to that when I have done with the States.
Now, as the master waits all night for the return of the Slave that
has run away from him, seeing, in the morning, he is absent, he
goes over to his neighbor's house, and asks him to look out for
him. Says he, "I went to town yesterday after my paper, and
when I had gotten it, I saw a statement of the organization of an
Abolition Convention, resolving that Slavery was a sin, and a reproach upon any free people, and that they would never desist
from its agitation, until they had eradicated the last string that
bound it to the country. I, of course, became somewhat grum
when I saw it; and, on going to the field, after getting home, in
that grum state, I, perhaps, might have been too much vexed to
have judged correctly the amount of work that should have been
done. I, at any rate, thought they had not done enough, and
scolded Tom for not having done more; he commenced muttering,
which only added fuel to the fire already kindled within me; so I
was in a bad fix to take his insolence, and made at him, when he
ran away. I would like to get hold of him, for if any of those
Abolitionists should happen to get hold of him, they would carry
him off."

Now, let us hear the consolation of his neighbor. He says:
"Yes; and let me tell you what happened at my house last Sun-
day. As I was going to the lot, I saw my Bob have a newspaper,
reading very attentively; and, on going to him, and asking him
to let me see it, I found that he was reading the paper that had
the very same proceedings of that Convention of the Abolitionists you were speaking of. So I lurked around my negroes' houses that night, to see if I could hear Bob say anything about the
Convention to the other negroes; and, sure enough I did, for I
heard him tell them that they would not be Slaves much longer,
for the Abolition party intended to set them all free, at the risk of

their lives. He was going on at a terrible rate; and, on peeping through a crack, I saw two of Mr. Jones' boys there too. So I slipped back to the house, and thought I would watch their manœuvres the next morning; and when morning came, I found them to be dull, careless, and very slothful. So I took them up, and whipped every one of them, and gave Bob two hundred lashes; then I got on my horse and rode over to Mr. Jones', and told him what I had heard Bob say in the presence of his two boys, and what I had done to mine. He called up his two boys and whipped them too. So you see how the thing is shaping. We must have our property protected against this diabolical set of Abolitionists, and our Legislatures must give us more power over our Slaves. And any man that will not agree to make the laws more binding on Slaves, can't get my vote, nor any one else that I can in the least influence."

Thus, they extort from their candidates a promise to legislate on the laws regulating the privileges of Slaves. The question is argued before the House, and, in the course of their argument, this circumstance of Bob's reading the paper is fully detailed, and hence proceeds the law prohibiting Slaves to be taught to read in this State. Now, it is not all astonishing to me to see this law so vigorously enforced, when aided by such an allied army of fiends as you Abolitionists are.

Well, kind reader, leaving the States, we will take a short view of the modern party that call themselves Republicans. They deny the name of Abolitionists, and call themselves the only true Republican party now existing, who, consequently, must be *right*. But when we view the treason of John Brown at Harper's Ferry, we must beg leave to pause for a moment, at least. But think not that I shall undertake to detail the attempt of Brown's treason, for that would be more than I could do, had I the wisdom of a Solomon, the expertness of a Byron or the discrimination of a Webster. The horror lying at the bottom of that attempt is more than I could describe. All I could say would not change its position before the people. My nerves would not suffer me to write it down, were I calculated to do so. Therefore, I can give you nothing but my imagination. I can imagine that I see gibbets all over the Slave-holding States, with negroes stretched upon them like slaughtered hogs, and pens of lightwood on fire! Methinks I hear their screams—I can see them upon their knees, begging, for God's sake, to have mercy. I can see them chained together by scores, and shot down like wild beasts. These are but shadows to what would have been done, had John Brown succeeded in his plan of getting up a rebelllion among the Slaves. Yet, these gentlemen say they have nothing to do with Slavery in the States. It would be hard to give you a correct account of these fanatics, were I not in possession of the Inaugural Address of the Governor of the State of Ohio, delivered January 9, 1860. I take it for granted that he must be a leading character of the would-be-called Republican party, by his majority. I shall detail what he says on the Slavery question—*i. e.*, the most prominent points; and I shall, at the same time, offer an abridged commentation throughout the address.

Hear him. He says: "On the subject of Slavery, the people of this State occupy no equivocal position." (All hands and the cook Abolitionists.) "They reject the modern dogma, that Slavery is essential to Republics, that such systems must fail without it, and that Slavery must be extended and perpetuated to extend and perpetuate our form of Government." But, in opposition to it, they have deliberately declared "that, in their judgment, Slavery is a pernicious wrong, and that patriotism and humanity unite in demanding their resistance to its extension into any free Territory, now, or that may be owned by the United States."

See what he says next: "They deny the binding authority of the dictum of the Supreme Court of the United States, asserting a right of property in one man over another, as a fundamental principle, and making the Federal Constitution the instrument of rendering it universal, as not limited to the reach of the local power which created the relation of master and Slave; but, on the contrary, we declare that the idea that there could be property in men was expressly excluded from the Constitution; which contains no such words as Slave, or Slavery, in any of its provisions, and in which every clause construed, or that can be construed, as referring to Slavery, regards it as the creature of State legislation, and dependent wholly upon State legislation for its existence and continuance."

Now, let us see what this means. He calls the decision of the Supreme Court a dictum, which, if his party had made, he would have called a *dictus!* He don't think it right to abide by it; notwithstanding it was referred to that Court, and owns to its authority to decide. He wants the Territories shaped in such a manner that he can carry his hogs there, but don't want a South-

erner to carry his slaves there.   He don't want Slavery to be tolerated, because the Constitution don't say Slave or Slavery.

"They deny that the Constitution guarantees to the Slavehold-
ing States any other than their local rights, in connection with the
use of Slavery, but such as it expressly declares : First, that the
Foreign Slave Trade should not be abolished before 1808 ; second,
that any law or regulation which any State might establish in favor
of Freedom, should not impair the legal remedy supposed at the
time of the adoption of the Constitution to exist by Common
Law for the reception, by legal process, in such States, of Fugitives from labor or service, escaping from other States ; and, third,
that three-fifths of all Slaves should be counted, in settling the
basis of representation in the several States.   Beyond these, the
framers of the Constitution intended to make no peculiar conces-
sions to the Slave-holding States, and these were made because
they had a Union of the States to create; and, to their ardent
and generous minds, the voluntary removal of Slavery by the
actions of the States themselves, without Federal interference,
seemed not only certain but close at hand.   The people of Ohio
have further declared that in their opinion, the people of a Territory have no power under the Constitution, or from any other
legal source, to establish Slavery as one of their institutions during their Territorial existence ; that the exercise of such a power
would be a manifest usurpation of the individual rights of the
citizens of the Territories, and utterly subversive of all popular
sovereignty, which demands, as a primary essential condition, the
recognition of inalienable personal rights.   They insist, also, that
coupled with the power is the duty of Congress to prohibit, by
express enactment, the extension of slavery into any Free Territory of the United States—that the exercise of this power has
been repeatedly approved of by every department of the State
and National Government, and to the universal acceptance of the
people, and that its recognition as a fundamental principle to be
hereafter exercised, whenever occasion may be presented, is indispensable to restore the simplicity and purity of the Government,
and to carry out the great purposes of the Constitution as declared in its preamble : to form a more perfect Union, to establish
justice, insure domestic tranquility, promote the general welfare,
and secure the blessings of liberty to ourselves and our posterity.
Such are the judgment of the people of Ohio, repeatedly expressed, on the subject of Slavery, as a social and political question."

3

Well, kind reader, we will see how we can interpret this part of the Constitution ourselves. The Governor has made the best job of it he could, I reckon; but I think the Constitution has as much right to protect the Georgian's property as it has the Ohioan's. The Governor may think a hog that would cost him $20 would be of more importance than a Slave that would cost $1,000 in Georgia. If the Governor thinks the Constitution meant only to protect Slavery in the States, where it then existed, why did they not cut short the importation of African Slaves at once, for you say all the Slave-holding States, at that time, were in the act of abolishing Slavery? I can tell you, Governor, why it was, because the people had found the Northern clime was not congenial with the African's nature, and, having but little Territory South at that time, thought it best to free their Slaves, as they were only an expense; but the framers of the Constitution, knowing that there would be Southern Territory as soon as the country could get properly on her feet, granted the continuance of the importation of African Slaves up to 1808. How can you say, Governor, that the framers of the Constitution never intended to protect Slavery, as well as any other species of property? Is it not specified in the Constitution what unlawful proceedings consist of? If they had intended that Slavery should not be carried beyond the limits it then had, they certainly would have left some signs, as they did in other things that they did not want practiced nor imposed upon their citizens—as in the case of attainder and *ex post facto* laws. If they did not intend that Congress should protect Slavery, they should have cut it off from the Constitution, and made it a separate law; for, as it now stands, it is included in that clause regulating the individual rights of all property owned in any part of the Union by its citizens.

Again, you say that, coupled with the power, is the duty of Congress to prohibit, by express enactment, the extension of Slavery into any Territory of the United States, thereby giving Congress the exclusive power to prohibit Slavery in a Territory, without the power to protect it. Now, we will suppose a case: Suppose a man from any Territory belonging to the United States should come to Ohio and take one of your hogs, and the State authorities should fail to indemnify your losses, where would you look, and who to, for an indemnity? Would you not either carry it to Congress or to the Supreme Court? I think you certainly would. But if the same man take a slave, the master has no right, outside of his State, to claim indemnity; so here goes a loss of at least $1,000, for want of the protection of Congress; whereas you have the right to recover $20 for your hog by the very same authority unto which the Southern Slaveholder has as much right to look for protection as you have. It then follows, what is the cause of this difference? I answer, it is founded in the false conception of your party in regard to the Constitutional claim of the Africans residing in the United States. Well, we must endeavor to see what that Constitutional claim is. We all know that the Constitution of the United States never has, since its formation, recognized the African as one of its citizens. The word Freedom does not necessarily imply citizenship, for, were that the case, all foreign emigrants would become citizens as soon as they landed, (Africans excepted,) for, by the Constitution, they are free. And there are hundreds of free persons here, but that don't make them citizens. If Freedom constitutes citizenship, it is something strange to me that the laws of your Free State (Ohio) prohibits a man being entitled to suffrage, if it can be proven that he has one drop of Negro blood in him. And I have seen twice, in the newspapers, where colored men, emigrating from other States into the State of Illinois, were taken up and sold into slavery for a length of time, sufficient to raise the sum of fifty dollars, to indemnify the State against the violation of a law prohibiting colored people entering that State. It is true, you can extend the citizenship of your State to any class you please, but that don't make it a Constitutional law of the United States.

The 6th Article of the Constitution of Liberia holds that, "Inasmuch as the essential object of its foundation was to offer an asylum for the scattered and oppressed children of Africa, and at the same time to regenerate the people of the vast continent of Africa, yet enveloped in the darkness of ignorance, none but persons of color will be allowed to become citizens of the Republic." Well, suppose the laws of that Republic recognized Slavery in some of its counties, would you be exempt from Slavery then? If the State of Ohio was at war with Kentucky, and the Kentuckians were to conquer you, and a vessel from Liberia was ready to sail, and the Kentuckians should take you to the ship and sell you to the Liberians, would you be their lawful property, or not? And when the ship arrived in Liberia, you not being entitled to suffrage, what kind of a position would you be in? I answer, you would be subject to sale; and any citizen of Liberia buying you, would hold you to Slavery for life, or during the confederation of the counties, or the duration of the Constitution. But there is another clause in the Constitution of the United States, that crowns all others in relation to Slaves being subjects of commerce, and that is: when the framers of the Constitution were regulating duties on foreign commerce, they laid, and commanded to be levied, $10 on each person imported for service into this Republic. Now, if that don't constitute the African a commercial piece of property, I am at a loss to know what commerce means.

In considering these facts, the Slave-holder only asks the protection of his property in any of the States or Territories subject to the Constitution of the United States, and this only amounts to an equality. This is what their Representatives are instructed to demand; and this is what, and all, they have demanded. The Southern members of Congress have always contended for this, and no more. But when they are sternly told that they cannot get it, it is enough to drive them to dissolution. Mark, what I say to you, citizens of Ohio, whenever this Union is dissolved, and the Slave-holders have cut loose entirely their commercial connection with you, there is no State in the Union that can, or will, feel it more forcibly than yourselves. Mark it, and keep it in your mind, that when the amount of pork and bacon sold to, and consumed by, Southern Slave-holders are cut short, you will then see what advantage the Slave-holder is to you. When we view the quantity of pork and bacon shipped from Cincinnati to the several intermediate points between there and New Orleans, you had better take care that your poor are not worse off than if they were living in Slave States. I, therefore, leave the subject with you, hoping that you may consider and reconsider it, and, at last desist from your agitation, and allow the Slave-holder his rights in the Union, and thereby cheat the spirit of Dissolution.

Kind reader, I suppose you have come to the conclusion, by this time, that I do not intend to recur to the Governor's Inaugural any more. Well, I have concluded about the same thing; for, as his views are before the country, and as they are hostile to the well-being of the Slave all the way through, and as the Governor has taken such a winding course to prove the non-protection of the Slave-holders, by the executive power, I shall only recur to his views at intervals.

Now, I will give you my candid opinion as regards the Black Republican party. It may seem harsh to them, but, in my opinion, it must inevitably work out that way, unless prevented by Divine agency. I hold that they are contaminated as regards the Dissolution of the Union; notwithstanding their contemptuous manner of speaking of the Slave-holder. For well do they know that it is the agitation of Slavery which is driving the Southern people to the necessity of doing such a thing. Well do they know the Southerners' whole peculiar and dependent interests are in his Slaves. According to an old proverb, "Touch a man's pocket, and you touch his heart." Now, the Black Republicans, knowing the Slave-holder's whole interest to be connected with Slavery, make war on that point, in order to force the Southern States to secede, that they may have the honor of remaining in the Union as the only true citizens. Nor would this satisfy them; for all know, that after the Southern States may have withdrawn from the Union, and divested themselves of the right of protection by the Federal Government, the spirit of innovation and encroachment would not only grow rampant, but new incentives would be given to insurrectionary movements against a people no longer their brethren in the Union. Notwithstanding they know that their officious interference between master and servant will but increase the bonds of the servant; and notwithstanding they know that the intelligent portion of the Slaves of the South thank them not for their pretended sympathy, yet they will still presume upon the influence which they think they can have upon the more ignorant and credulous of our race, by promising them a rich and flourishing country in Central or South America. But let the non-participation of the Slaves, at the Harper's Ferry treason teach them a lesson of Negro feelings in the South. This was but the A B C; if they will try it again, they will get to *the pictures*.

I have no doubt, in my mind, but such a state of things would follow a dissolution of the Union, for Governor Dennison, of Ohio, in his Inaugural, of January the 9th, 1860, urged, emphatically, the acquisition of Central America, or some portion of South America, for a settlement of the free colored people of this country and Africa. And as we see the late attempt of John Brown, who, from all accounts, was one of their leading men, how can we doubt, for one moment, the above conclusions? It does seem that Brown's failure to instil into the breast of the Slaves rebellious notions, ought to be a lesson for the balance of the fanatics; but I would not trust them on their oats, unless I had them in manacles so that I could retain them for punishment. But just let them march their motley corps into the Slave-holding States, expecting the aid of the Slaves, and they will find that the old Brown's gibbet will confront many a one of them. I tell you, fanatics, the Slaves of the Southern States are getting too old to be humbugged by your eternal cry of *freedom!* They have heard it too much, and felt the effects too often, to be gulled any more. I would to God that every Slave had the discrimination to view your position, and your motives, in their proper light. But they know enough now, by severe experience, growing out of your infernal agitation, to enable them to resist any attempt you may make to persuade them to rebel against their masters. You must recollect, fanatical sirs, that the Slave children and their young masters and mistresses, are all raised up together. They suck together, play together, go a hunting together, go a fishing together, go in washing together, and, in a great many instances, eat together in the cotton-patch, sing, jump, wrestle, box, fight boy fights, and dance together; and every other kind of amusement that is calculated to bolt their hearts together when grown up. You had better mind how you come here and jump aboard of our masters; for I tell you, though we sometimes fight among ourselves, if another man jumps on either, we both pitch into him. You must recollect that we are not oppressed here like your nominally free there. We can go into our masters' houses and get plenty of good things to eat; and we can shake hands with the big-bugs of the country, and walk side-by-side with Congress members on the side-walks, and stand and converse with gentlemen of the highest rank, for hours at a time. So, in short, we can do anything, with the exceptions of those privileges wrested from us in consequence of your diabolical, infernal, Black Republican, Abolition, fanatical agitation.

But, perhaps, you will say, in the face of all this, "our colored people are not subject to a separation from their families, as the Slaves are; for when they marry they have the same chance to live and remain with their families as we do, for we have no law to separate them." That all may be; but when we consider the many deprivations the colored man is subject to in a country granting him these lawful privileges, we would wonder that the colored man is held in such low esteem, were it not that we are posted on the social relations in which he stands in the non-Slave-holding States, it is a common thing to see poor, half-naked, and starving creatures, standing on corners, begging every one passing by for a penny. And it is not at all surprising, when we consider the prejudice existing there against them. As for myself, I would rather have the law against me, and prejudice in my favor, than to have the law in my favor and the prejudice against me. For the decisions of the law are always, in a greater or less degree, subject to prejudice. The colored man is a colored man anywhere. He is but the tool North, and the servant South.

Perhaps the reader has not forgotten what I stated in the first of this address. I there stated that Slavery consisted in the absolute power one individual had over another. It matters not from what source this power is derived; it is all the same with the subordinate, with the single exception that the Slave is a Slave for life, with a master that is bound, by the laws, to protect him; and the other, a subordinate for life, with no protection. So you see, the Slave has some one that is pecuniarily interested in his welfare, who, therefore, extends to him every advantage that will preserve and augment longevity; whereas, the other is in a subordinate condition, in a climate that is not congenial to his health, and no one to care for him. He is restricted to this climate, too, without any thing, or any person, or power, to protect him, other than the common law, and that being over-powered by prejudice against him, buries him in infamy never to rise, only at the option of the oppressor. So, viewing these circumstances in their proper light, I would rather have my wife sold ten thousand miles from me, with a master that I knew was bound by the laws, and his interest, to protect her and the children, than to be with her and the children without food, and no way under God's heaven to make it —sitting in some damp cellar, almost stifled with the stench arising from the putrefaction and filth; there, sitting and shivering, with scarcely clothing sufficient to hide their nakedness, and nothing to eat. This is a nice fix to leave your colored people in, in the North, to come here and make war upon Slave-holders! It is, indeed!

But the Governor, in his Inaugural, says: "Slavery is detrimental to the poor whites; for," says he, "the poor whites having no land nor Slaves, are reduced to Slavery themselves." A contradiction to that statement would be unnecessary, as every body, in this section, knows that the poor whites are ten times better off here than in the non-Slaveholding States; and the every-day occurrence of their emigrating from there here, is a positive proof without any further comment.

With all the facts stated above, in regard to the constitutionality of Slavery, that party has but one more prop to sustain them, and that is William H. Seward's claims on the Higher Law. Well, you must watch me very closely in dealing with this subject, for I consider it of more importance than the whole of the United States.

That there is a Higher Law of Supreme Power, and that to this Power, kingdoms, empires, principalities, republics, and all other potentials, are subject, and ought to fall down before Him and do homage, is without a doubt. But in order to arrive at a correct understanding of this Law, it is our indispensable duty to calculate the greatest possible happiness to mankind generally. For, without taking it in a general sense, we might confine it to the narrow precincts of our selfish conceptions. I will now give my views of the Higher Law.

I contend that the circumstance of Melchisedeck meeting Abraham in the wilderness, and blessing him, and giving him bread and wine, emblematic of the body and blood of our Lord and Savior Jesus Christ, was a manifestation of the Higher Law. I contend that the blindness of Isaac, which caused him to be cheated into the bestowal of the blessing upon Jacob instead of Esau, was a manifestation of the Higher Law. I contend that the circumstance of Jacob having to flee from the wrath of Esau to a foreign land, and his ultimate marriage with Rachel, thus establishing the lineage of the Messiah, was a manifestation of the Higher Law. I contend that the circumstance of Joseph being sold as a slave into Egypt, and his subsequent elevation to power and consequence among the Egyptians, was a manifestation of the Higher Law. I contend that the circumstance of Moses, in consequence of the edict of Pharaoh, being placed in a rush cradle and taken thence into the care and education of the King's daughter, thereby fitting him for the course of his after life, was a manifestation of the Higher Law. I contend that the circumstance of Moses' slaying the Egyptian, and having to flee to the wilderness, in which he was afterwards to wander, was a manifestation of the Higher Law. I contend that the circumstance of David having placed Uriah in the front of the battle, where he was slain, thus enabling himself to raise, by Bathsheba, a legitimate son, who was to be endowed with wisdom above all men, was a manifestation of the Higher Law. I contend that the overthrow of Jerusalem, by the wicked and idolatrous Nebuchadnezzar, and the carrying away of the children of Israel to Babylon, affording them an opportunity of embracing the true Religion, was a manifestation of the Higher Law. I contend that the death and resurrection of Jesus Christ, and the redemption of fallen man, was a manifestation of the Higher Law. I contend that the circumstance of the primitive Christians having to flee into the wilderness, with the Holy Bible under their arms, in order to escape the persecution of the then chaotic world, thereby saving the Bible, with other valuable histories, was a manifestation of the Higher Law. I contend that the circumstance of the Africans being sold to the Europeans, and from them to the Americans, as Joseph was to the Egyptians, thereby bringing them into a land flowing, as it were, with the milk and honey of the Gospel, making them familiar with a code of laws not to be surpassed by those of any nation on earth; extending religious liberty to all, fitting them for teachers in the various precepts of civilization, morality and religion, so necessary in the establishment of enlightened and Christian society; fitting them for useful missionaries to their benighted brethren in Africa, thereby preparing the way for the glad shout of "Hallelujah to God and the Lamb" in benighted Africa, is a manifestation of the Higher Law.

Reader, I expect your patience is somewhat threadbare; but I have been thus particular, in order to show *Mr. William H. Seward* my views on the subject which he seems to base the whole of his strength upon. I shall present a short, statistical account of the Slave Trade, and wind up. I quote from good authority:

"It is estimated, that in the city of New York, alone, about twelve vessels are fitted out every year, for the Slave Trade; and that Boston and Baltimore furnish, each, about the same number, making a fleet of thirty-six vessels. If to these be added the Slavers fitted out in other Eastern ports, besides Boston, we will have a total of about forty, which is rather under than over the actual number. Each Slaver registers from 150 to 250 tons, and costs, when ready for sea, with provisions, Slave equipments, and everything necessary for a successful voyage, about $8,000. There, to start with, we have a capital of $320,000, the greater part of which is contributed by Northern men."

A writer on the subject, states the amount of capital vested in the course of a year, and says that the men engaged in it receive a profit beyond belief. And there is no doubt but most of the men engaged in it are those fanatics who make the most fuss about Slavery.

Now, my Northern brethren, if you are so philanthropic in our cause as you pretend to be, you can bestow your kindnesses on those poor creatures who are not acquainted with our laws and customs; you can concentrate your whole force against those lawless vandals, who purchase for speculation and sell for gain, without interrupting us, who are far better off than they are. But that would not answer your purpose, for you are not law-abiding citizens, though you pretend to be all the ones that are. If you could get in power, and buy or steal Central America, and place your freed or stolen colored brethren there, you would then have things as you want them; for it would not be long before some Slave would be endeavoring to get over where he could be "*free indeed;*" and on demanding them, the Slave-holder would, inevitably, be insulted, which would produce anarchy, which would naturally draw in your fanatical party, and W. H. Seward, straddling his hobby—Higher Law nag—would march at the head of his party into Central America, and form an alliance with the Central Americans, and march the allied forces against the Slave-holding States, and utterly overthrow them, and set up a monarchial government, and crown William H. Seward king.

I am of the opinion, that if the conservative men of this Republic do not concentrate the two great national parties, and form a redoubt, and stay within its precincts, you will never rue it but once, and that will be all your lifetime. Hence, in this enlightened and (ought to be) patriotic Republic, where the people are their own king, their own emperor, their own monarch, having one of the sublimest forms of government in existence, to suffer a set of diabolical fanatics to be the instruments of an overthrow of their much-honored country, would render them a hissing and a by-word for every nation, and an everlasting stigma upon the wisdom and patriotism of its citizens.

Having viewed this subject in what I conceive to be the proper light, I now proceed to prove it to be true. And, in order to do that, I shall have to lay before you the inconsistency of the Abolition cause. They pretend to be governed by the Higher Law principle, which, they say, teaches the inestimable right, guaranteed to all men, to govern themselves nationally, domestically and personally. Well, we will view this subject, but while we most emphatically acknowledge, that all men were, originally, born free, we are constrained to acknowledge the power of Him who created all things out of nothing, to change any part of His creation as best suits Him; or, in other words, change original things so that they may be productive of the greatest amount of good to mankind, generally. This I mentioned in my preliminary remarks upon the Higher Law. I only mention it again to lay a basis sufficiently impregnable to enable me to refute their pretensions to the claims which all men have upon that Law. Now, it matters not what, or how, a thing was in the creation, nor so long as we have reason to believe that the continuance of the original, or the change as we find them, was caused by the Creator of the thing Himself. So, under this consideration, I hold that both the *original* and the *change* are constitutionally right, for we read, in the beginning, that man was happy, and had nothing to do but eat, drink, and be lord of all he surveyed; and, that, too, without an effort on his part, to provide for the same. But mark the sequel: after he transgressed, he was driven out of the garden, and forced to manual labor for a sustenance. We cannot say it was wrong in the Creator, for man did it himself.

Well, we have *one* change caused by the created. Now let us hunt up another. I shall only note two others, as I have spoken at some length on this subject above. But I must mention here, before going further, that the Creator works by means and instrumentalities, so that whatsoever He commands, or authorizes His faithful servants to do, is ratified at His tribunal, and, consequently, is as legitimate as if He had done it Himself.

The next circumstance I shall present to refute this claim on the Higher Law, is the case of Noah and his sons. We read in the ninth chapter of Genesis that after the waters abated, Noah set himself to till the earth; and after having raised a good crop and made much wine, he drank of the same, and was made drunk. His clothes being displaced, his younger son saw his nakedness and laughed at him. Now, when Noah knew it, he was angry, and in that mood he pronounced the first curse of servitude. Certainly, this must be another departure from the original Higher Law claims, for Ham was as free born as Shem and Japhet, yet we see that Shem and Japhet were to dwell together, and poor Ham had to serve them. I wonder if there were any agitators, or abolitionists, then to kick up a fuss with Noah, about making a Slave of his son? and with his two brothers for making him work for them? I guess not, for I don't think the devil had that much power so soon after the flood. We will now proceed to the other circumstance.

We read in the ninth chapter of Joshua, that when the Israelites found that they were deceived by the men of Gibeon, they were sore displeased, but, in consequence of their oaths, they could not slay them as they had done others. But mark the sequel: they were constituted perpetual servants to the children of Israel as hewers of wood and drawers of water. So we see, in these few instances, that the claim on the Higher Law will not do; and men having the confidence of their respective States to enable them to become legislators for the people at large, holding forth such doctrines to the ignorant classes of the United States, are guilty of blasphemy against God and the Constitution, and are, most emphatically, contaminated with dangerous deceit.

It is enough to know, that such are entitled to citizenship, but when they are placed at the head of Government, we may well quake with fear.

I will now endeavor to show how the course of these fanatics affects things generally. I shall prove that, according to their own interpretation of the Constitution, there is property in man; for they admit this fact, that the Constitution recognizes an inferiority in the Slave where it says that three-fifths of all slaves shall be taken in settling the basis of Representative population. Here, they must acknowledge an inferiority, for it takes five slaves to make three white men. The next instance we see, is the certainty that the framers of the Constitution recognized property in man. This we can easily do from these three clauses: The first is, where it says fugitives from service, escaping into another State, shall be rendered up to the rightful owner, on the demand of the same. The next is, a levy of ten dollars' tax on all persons imported into this country for service. The third is, the prohibition of the importation of persons held to service in 1808. Well, let us now consider the probability of these three clauses. We find the first acknowledging an inferiority in the Slave. I would like for the Abolitionists to tell me why that was done. But as they are not present I shall have to answer for them: My opinion is, that as the Africans never emigrated to this country, but were brought here and sold as Slaves—they being found in that condition at the formation of the Constitution, they were left in the same condition. Now, as the right to property is inherent in all things coming to him through that channel, it then follows that those who had invested their all in Slaves, had the right to hold and demand the rendition of them, when fled from service into another State, with the same propriety as a brother of his had to demand his horse, or any other species of property. I think the other two clauses need no comment, for they explain themselves. Let us suppose a case: Suppose you, or any of you, were, or are, mechanics, and had an apprentice bound to you to learn a trade, after you had been bound by law to support and protect him comfortably, during his apprenticeship, would it be law in the same law not to give you power to hold him as your rightful property during his term of apprenticeship? And would it not be right for you to demand him, anywhere in the United States in case he should run away? And if you had the right to do so, would that not constitute the right of property in him during his term of apprenticeship? I think it would. Well, if the Southerner, by hard labor and strict economy, saves money enough in five or six years to buy a Slave, and the same should run away and get into a Free State, can not he demand his rendition of the authorities of that State, by the Constitution? This you acknowledge was the true meaning of the clause, and if it is, will not that constitute property in man? It is impossible for you to dodge this question, for your Black Republican Governor of Ohio, in his Inaugural, admitted that that was the meaning of the fugitive clause.

This being true, how can you say the decision of the Supreme Court is not a final adjustment of the Slavery question? You say, indirectly, that the rendition of fugitives, escaping from service, is constitutional, but turn right to the opposite side, and say that the Constitution does not recognize property in man. What folly! what folly!! A ten year old boy, born and raised in Georgia, would know better than to lay claim to a piece of property that he could not prove to be his by the laws of the State. I know you must see the inconsistency of your course; but that you care nothing about. All you care for, is to provoke the Southerners to anger, so as to get them divided far enough apart to admit your factional bandits. Your schemes have been ingeniously laid, and they are working harmoniously; but I am in hopes, and do earnestly pray, that the conservative men will become sensitive, and awake in time to defeat your sectional fanaticism, by rallying around one of the conservative candidates for the Presidency. For the election of a Black Republican to that office, would put manacles on every Slave south of Mason and Dixon's line. Even now the oppression has commenced, but where it will end God only knows.

Who are you, who call yourselves my friends? who cause me

to be ten times worse oppressed, by your pretended friendship?
Who are you, who say that all men, by the teaching of the Higher Law, should be free? when, at the same time, that very Law
contradicts it, and shows, conclusively, that from the earliest pe-
riod to the present day, one man was commanded to serve the
other. Who are you, who deny that persons have been born
Slaves prior to the enslavement of the Africans in America? when
St. Paul said, nearly two thousands years ago, when speaking to
a multitude of feud makers, such as you are, that he was *free-
born ;* showing, most conclusively, that all men *were not so born*
in his day. Who are you, who say that the oppression of the
Slaves of the South, is the prime cause of your sympathy? when
you know that your pretended sympathy oppresses the Slave tenfold more. Who are you, who hate your brother Southerner, and
accuse him of bringing reproach and disgrace upon the Republic?
when he is actually doing more for the protection of the country
than you are, for, whereas, you employ men to work in your man-
ufactories until you are overwhelmed with wealth, made on the
labor of the poor men working for such small wages, barely sufficient to keep them comfortable while in the bloom of youth.
What becomes of them when bowed down with old age, without
a penny in their pockets? Are they not thrown on the public?
Suppose this money, that is taken to support them, were paid into
the public treasury, would it not lessen the national debt, which is
now forty-five* millions of dollars? Who pays the physician's
bill of a poor man and his family, if taken sick while working for
you at a shilling a day? Do you take the money that they have
made for you to pay their expenses? or do you drive them out of
your house into a hospital, to be taken care of by the State until
they sufficiently recover their health, and go to work for you again?
Thus you receive all meat and no bones ; for you get all the poor
man's labor, without incurring any risk whatever, by throwing the
expenses on the State. The country is impoverished at the expense of your aggrandizement; but, on the other hand, the Southerner only gets the labor of his Slave by paying all expenses during his youthful days, and when he is old and unable to work, he
is bound, by the laws of his section, to take care of him with the
same money he earned when young. Now, after supporting him
during his health, if the Slave should happen to become insane,
the authorities would grumble like thunder and lightning to have

---

*It is now, in 1861, some sixty millions of dollars.

the insane Slave thrown on their hands. They would say, that the owner ought to take care of him. This looks like bringing reproach and disgrace on the Republic, don't it? If you would pay attention to the domestic affairs in your own States, it would be more beneficial to your section, and less annoyance to the South.

With these views before you, I cannot see what grounds you can have to meet and nominate a candidate for the Presidency of the United States, when you know that the President takes an oath that compels him to know no North, no South, no East, and no West. How can he take the oath of fidelity to all sections of the Union, when he is nominated and placed on a sectional platform, which says, in its embodiment of principles, that, coupled with the power, it is the duty of Congress to prohibit, by express enactment, the extension of Slavery into any of the Territories belonging to the United States? Let us view this matter a little. Suppose that in a short time after his inaugural, a Territory should offer herself to Congress for admission with a pro-Slavery Constitution, a majority of its citizens wishing it, what could you do with that petition? what can you promise the people you would do with it? If you were to reject it, you would show that you were not carrying out the principles demanded by the Constitution, and if you were to receive it, you would violate the pledge made to your factional party, who say it is the duty of Congress to prohibit the extension of Slavery into the Territories. So what would you do? If I may be permitted to answer, I say that my opinion is, you would reject the offer, with the pro-Slavery Constitution, upon the Higher Law claims. That not being recognized by the conservative members, Congress would be thrown into anarchy, and cry out encroachment! encroachment!! Out of this would be sent up one eternal cry for equal rights! equal rights! On this being denied the conservative members, what else could be expected than the dissolution of the Union, and the government destroyed? The anarchy in Congress would go with the velocity of a planet; and like the vapor rising from malarious districts, would diffuse itself in every hole and corner of the United States, and dampen the prospects of every conservative man. The last ray of light being exhausted from their hopes, they would be left no alternative, but to unsheath the sword against their brothers, for the protection of their rights. The final result of these proceedings it is not with me to say, but look at it, you factionists, and see if you can not prophesy as Ezekiel did of Jerusalem.

To MASTERS AND THEIR SLAVES.—Masters, I most beseechingly wish you to read the following to your Slaves, and tell them it is the request of one that is their brother in bondage. For I believe, if the Slaves were undeceived respecting their chance of enjoying freedom, any where within the incorporate limits of the United States, or, in fact, any where on the continent of North America, they would not change places with the poor white man North. But while they are deceived in believing that they are worse off, and worse treated, than any one else, it is natural that they should be dissatisfied. But if you remove this gloom from over their eyes, and enable them to see, not only their true position, but, also, that of the millions of the poor and oppressed, not only in Europe, Asia and Africa, but in the Northern States of America; and if hundreds of them, on plantations, even knew how hard run some are in the Southern cities to live comfortable, they could see, clearly, that their enslavement, under all circumstances by which it is surrounded, is not such a curse as they thought it was. After they become convinced that their position is better than four-fifths of mankind, they will cast aside all foolish hopes of bettering their condition, and be enabled to view the four-fifths of the laboring population of the country as being in a far worse condition than they are themselves. This would create within them a satisfaction with their lots sufficient to make them trustworthy in the most difficult times.

To MY BROTHER SLAVES.—Brethren, let us reason together. I expect to prove to you, in a very few words, that Slavery existed thousands of years ago, and that it was a lawful institution long before the enslavement of the Israelites. We read in the 14th chapter and 14th verse of Genesis, that Abraham numbered 318 servants, born in his own house. And we read again, in the same book, 50th chapter, 19th and 20th verses, where Joseph was speaking of his being sold into Egypt, that it was done to save much people alive. And, coming down to the Christian era, we find, all over the New Testament, admonitions to servants commanding them to obey their masters.

I will give one instance, sufficiently conclusive, without stating many, which would weary the mind. We read in Ephesians, the 6th chapter and 5th verse, as follows: "Servants, be obedient to them that are your masters, according to the flesh, with fear and trembling, in singleness of your hearts, as unto Christ; not with eye-service, as men-pleasers, but as the servants of Christ, doing the will of God from the heart; with good will doing service, as to the Lord, and not to men. Knowing that whatsoever good thing any man doeth, the same shall he receive of the Lord whether he be bond or free."

Now, this is sufficiently strong to show that St. Paul approved of Slavery; but this is only one out of hundreds, equally strong. Well, if we find Christ, and the Apostles favoring it, we must be very particular, or we might be found fighting against God. Now, my kind brethren in bondage, if it be so that the children of Israel were enslaved, for the express purpose of saving much people alive, how much more might it be possible that the Slaves of America are enslaved to save many Africans alive? They send us heathens, but we send them educated Ministers in return. Tell me which of the two do you believe to be right: The man who says he is your friend, but don't want you brought from the heathenish country, on account of your unworthiness to live with white men in an enlightened and religious country, or the one that says, "bring them on, we will receive them, for they naturally belong to a warm climate; and they, having no money to pay us for our trouble in teaching them the rudiments of the true religion, have to work, thereby fitting them both for agricultural and religious duties. We will let them work our farms, and we will be bound to take care of them, as long as they live." This rule is only applicable in the general acceptation of the term. I now notice it in a domestic point of view.

My brother Slave, let me ask you one question: Which do you think are our real, true friends, the Abolitionists, North, or our masters South? Perhaps I will have to lay the matter before you to enable you to answer. I look at in this light, that "where your treasure is, there will be your heart, also." This, I think, is easily proved by the natural disposition to love self best; for if you work hard and lay up money enough to buy a horse, it is natural to suppose that you will think more of him than a stranger would. You will, of course, feel interested in him, and will do all you can to render him comfortable.

I hold, that the master, having labored hard, and accumulated wo or three thousand dollars, and laying it out in Slaves, is entitled to their service. Don't it look natural for him to have more sympathy, growing out of an interest for them, than a man in New

York, or Ohio, who never saw you, but who is making a tremendous fuss about your welfare? Does it look reasonable for him to have as much real sympathy for you, as the man who has spent the whole earnings of a quarter of a century in purchasing you? This is the true feature of the case; our masters buy us with the money they have worked hard for, and, of course, they will look more to our interest than one who is not, in any shape or form, interested in us. And the Slave has another advantage: the laws of the South compel our masters to protect us against hunger, nakedness, or any other want of the necessaries of life. This is reasonable, and I hope you will view it in its proper light, so as to endear your masters to you as friends, and not make enemies of them. But if you doubt their being better friends to you than the Abolitionists are, I beg you to look, for a moment, at the effect their course of proceedings has upon your happiness and privileges. The Abolitionist will tell you that you ought to be free, and that if you will rise against your masters, they will help you. But look at them after they succeed in getting a few poor, ignorant Slaves to join them; they will push the Slaves forward; and when our masters are led to the light of what is going on, they commence abusing us. The Abolitionists being behind, make their escape, and leave us to take all the consequences. They know that we cannot get off, from the fact that we cannot travel without a pass. Now, to prove to you that they are our worst enemies, just see how they act, and that will convince you that they are the worst of all enemies to the Slave. For when they flee from the neighborhood, where they have excited a few foolish Slaves to rebellion, they go out of the reach of that neighborhood, and propagate their slanders anew, accusing masters of abusing and oppressing their Slaves. When they have effected an excitement in one neighborhood, and fled from it, they will endeavor to get up another excitement where they are. I wish to know, if any of you are so blind as not to see the inconsistency of their pretensions to the friendship of Slaves?

But, perhaps, some of you may say, that, in case they should succeed in getting off with you, you would be free. Just let me say to you, that as soon as you were landed on free soil, your pretended friend would have nothing more to do with you. He would tell you to go to work; but after you had tried in vain to get something to do, and failed, you would, perhaps, hunt him up, and tell him that you were without money, and could not get anything to do. He would point out some other place, and send you there; but after you had tried all over that neighborhood, and were told that they did not employ negroes while there was so many white men, with families, needing work; and that you had better go back to the man that brought you there; then you would begin to think that you had better staid where you had some one to give you plenty of work to do, and plenty of victuals to eat. And, more especially, would you feel the truth of what I say, when you went back to the man that had decoyed you off, and he being tired of your troubling him, *might* bring you a piece of meat and bread to the door, and handing it to you, drive you away from his house. Such treatment might do for those poor colored people there, who never knew any better, but it would not do for a Slave of the South, accustomed to being treated as a human being. So, whenever one talks to you about being free, tell him that you had rather stay where some one is compelled to take care of you, than to go where no one is, and where you are equally as subordinate as you would be where you had some one to protect you. In fact, I hold that the subordination of the poor colored man North, is greater than that of the Slave South.

Now, fanatical sirs, what authority have you to predict, for the American people, the acquisition of some portion of Central or South America, to settle the colored man upon, or the non-extension of Slave Territory? Are you the guardian Angel of the American Republic, sent from Heaven, to set forth what is right, and what is wrong? If you are, I think that Tribunal badly represented; for, instead of your teaching peace and harmony, you are laying the basis of a destruction of the Union. The continued feuds kept up in Congress, growing out of the agitation of the Slavery question, ought to be a lesson to any patriotic citizen, to let that question alone. And if you were truly patriotic citizens, you would *let it alone*.

Hoping that you will see the folly of your course, and turn to the spirit which actuated your forefathers, I bid you adieu. I ask your pardon for any misrepresentation I may have made, in regard to your intentions—but for nothing more.

I beg the pardon of all conservative Northern citizens for not separating them, in every instance, from the Abolitionists, in this address.

I beg the pardon of all Southerners, if I have said anything detrimental to their wishes.

I beg the pardon of all colored people, if I have said anything offensive to their feelings, hoping they will impute it to the sympathy I have for the oppressed and benighted of my people at large.

CRITICISM

ON

LINCOLN'S INAUGURAL.

GENTLE READER, I do not expect to develop to you anything new in this, my addition, other than my views on the Inaugural Address of the President of the remaining part of the United States. For it would be useless to look up abstract questions now to prove anything, while the position of the above named President is before us; for the die is cast, "the deed is done," a Black Republican is elected President. Yes! elected President of the United States. A sectional man—a fanatical man—a man that was nominated by a sectional and fanatical party, and placed upon a sectional and fanatical platform—this man we find a few days ago taking the oath of fidelity to all sections of the country. Notwithstanding, he said in his inaugural, a few minutes before he took this oath, that there were different opinions in regard to the extension of Slavery, which would naturally be as binding on him to give his aid in its extension, as in checking it. Is it possible that the American people will continue to suffer this diabolical faction to lead them on by degrees? Their mouths gape with that old Syrian song—

"Take time! take time!
Mind what you do!"

Is the election of an enemy, (and I liked to have said a sworn one,) to one section of the country, sufficient cause for the suffering section to withdraw from the other? If the Revolutionary fathers had danced to that tune, what would have been your condition to-day? Is the world stronger than the Almighty that formed it? or is the Constitution stronger than the people who made it? Reader, it is not my intention to say anything about the Constitution being unworthy the object for which it was formed; but that object being violated, it then follows that there is an aggressor somewhere; and if you succeed in finding him, and require of him an indemnity for the wrongs done to that instrument, it is his indispensable duty to adjust the matter amicably and satisfactory. And any selfish motive, sectional strife, party aggrandizement or fanatical factions, ought to debar the aggressor, if proven guilty of these one-sided principles, the privilege of presiding over that part of the section to which he was known to be an enemy. This conclusion brings with it the position occupied by the Republican party.

Let us hear what Mr. Lincoln says on this subject. He says : "Apprehension seems to exist among the people of the United States, that by the accession of a Republican administration, their property and their peace are to be endangered. There has never been any reasonable cause for such apprehension. Indeed, the most ample evidence has all the while existed, and been open to their inspection. It is found in all the published speeches of him who now addresses you. I do quote from one of those speeches, when I declare that I have no purpose, directly or indirectly, to interfere with the institution of Slavery in the States where it exists. I believe I have no lawful right to do so—and I have no inclination to do so."

Let us see how this will compare with the platform upon which the *honorable* gentleman was elected. The party that framed the platform, and placed him on it, vows vengeance to Slavery, and say that it is a pernicious sin, and that humanity and religion ought to demand its cessation. Under this head the party finds a pretext to back them in enacting laws to prohibit the rendition of fugitives escaping from service; and under this pretext they shelter themselves, when it is proven that the Constitution admits of Slavery being carried anywhere within the incorporate limits of the United States.

But let me return to the President's inaugural. He says : "Those who nominated and elected me, did so with knowledge that I had made this and many other similar declarations, and had never recanted them. And more than this, they placed in the platform for my acceptance, and as a law to themselves and to me, the clear and emphatic resolutions which I now read:

"'*Resolved*, That maintenance inviolate of the rights of the States, and especially the rights of each State, to order and control its domestic institutions according to its own judgment exclusively, is essential to that balance of power on which the perfection and endurance of our political fabric depends, and we denounce the lawless invasion, by armed force, of the soil of any State or territory—no matter under what pretext—as among the gravest crimes.' "

The President then goes on to say: "I now reiterate these sentiments, and in doing so, I only press upon the public attention the most conclusive evidence of which the case is susceptible. The property, peace and security of no section is to be in anyweis endangered by the incoming administration.

"I add, too, that all the protection which consistently with the Constitution and the laws, can be given, will be cheerfully given to all the States, when lawfully demanded for whatever cause—as cheerfully to one section as to the other."

We will see, by and by, what this self-delegated power intends to do with the seceding States. But here he goes:

"There is much controversy about the delivering up of fugitives from service or labor. The clause I now read it as plainly written in the Constitution as any other of its provisions: "No person held to service or labor in one State, under the laws thereof, escaping into another, shall, in consequence of any laws or regulations therein, be discharged from such service or labor, but shall be delivered on claim of the party to whom such service or labor may be due.' "

The *honorable* gentleman says, in regard to this, that—

"It is scarcely questioned that this provision was intended, by those who made it, for the reclaiming of fugitives Slaves, and the intention of the law-giver is the law. All members of Congress swear their support to the whole Constitution—to this provision as much as to any other. To the proposition, then, that Slaves whose cases come within the terms of this clause, shall be delivered up, their oaths are unanimous. Now, if they would make an effort in *good temper*, could they not, with an equal unanimity, make and pass a law by means of which to keep good that unanimous oath?"

The President acknowledges the right of each State to make and keep inviolate her own domestic regulations; but the party he represents denies the right of a Slave-holder to go into their Free States, and demand a fugitive Slave. Perhaps he would think it a bad affair, if a man from Georgia was to go into his State and steal $1,000 worth of property, and bring it to Georgia; and if he came after it, the authorities should tell the *honorable* gentleman that he had no business with it, and that he could not get it, he would feel pretty tolerable bad, I reckon. But, oh! the *honorable* gentleman says that they must make the effort in good temper. I declare I liked to have forgotten that. But I expect it is a pretty hard matter for a Georgian to keep in a very good humor, after he has paid $1,000 for a Slave, for him to run away (or be stolen) to a Free State, where he would have to carry with him another man, at his own expense; and after getting there, be indicted for slander, and a demand made of him to pay his Slave for what time he had owned him; and, if he get him at all, it might cost him more than the Slave was worth. I think it would be pretty hard for him to make the effort in good temper.

But the *President* says there is some little *difference* of opinion in regard to which authority, the State Executive, or the National, should be clothed with the power. But this, he says, is a matter of little consequence, since it matters not by what authority he gets his Slave. He also says the reason they make such a great fuss about it is, that they do not want to make a mistake, and take up a free man and give to the owner of the Slave. Poor fellow! you certainly must pay but little attention to your darkies there, if you don't know them living in your own towns.

But the President says that all demands shall be given up when lawfully made. But I reckon he don't think it lawful for a Georgian to take a witness to Ohio to prove a Slave to be his.

But I guess he will find it quite as unlawful, when he undertakes to coerce the seceding States back into the Union, upon the ground that they had no constitutional right to do so. Yet he says the intention of the law-giver is the law. He also admits that there is no clause in the Constitution more plainly written than the rendition of fugitives; and, in the face of all this, he has the hardihood to appear on the stage and there declare, in the face of the civilized world, his intention to coerce the seceding States back, when they have only withdrawn for the vindication of their rights, which have been trampled on for years; and, instead of getting better, it is getting worse.

It is true he may coerce them back, but it will be into their mother earth; but never will they be forced back into the Union, without a sufficient indemnity for the wrongs practised on them by your diabolical faction. Talk about holding the public property, and collecting the revenues! I suppose the property of the Southern States is not worth as much to her citizens as your would-be-called revenues. Now you pretend to be so very conservative, promising to administer the laws to all sections of the country with equal justice, no matter in what shape or form. Let me see if you can stand one test. You being a lawyer, it is an easy matter to answer the first question. Tell me, kind sir, what term of years are required for an act of misdemeanor, unappeased for, to become null and void? Does it not hold good against the offending party during the existence of the same? It certainly does. Well, you say that you don't wish to use any hostility to the South. If you don't, make this proposition to the Slave-holding States : that the old family records, together with the executives, and let there be a valuation according to the value of Slaves during that day down to the present time, and then compel the Free States to pay the valuation made by the Slave-holding States ; and you would do an act that would clothe you with more honor than all the Presidents of the United States, and would be a lasting fame that would not forsake you when you had long since mingled with your mother dust.

Now this request will never be made, of course, but it might be made with as much accuracy as could the Republican party expect the South to give up the property of their States, which had formerly belonged to the United States. For she has hundreds of thousands of dollars, no doubt, invested in Slaves now residing in the Free States ; and, what is more than all, the authorities of these States—nine* of them—have met and passed laws hostile to the Fugitive clause, which Mr. Lincoln says is as plainly written as any other clause in the Constitution. Nevertheless, the people have passed these laws, and in order to give them all the force that could be given to law, they have made it a criminal offence to assist in any way in recapturing a fugitive. I don't recollect the exact penalty, but I think it is ten year's imprisonment and $1,000 fine, in the most of the States.

The President, in treating of this *very delicate* matter, said that the Fugitive Law was as well executed as well could be, and that a few would break over any law. Now this kind of talk might do, had it been a few citizens of a State, but when we find an over-whelming majority, so much so, that they made it the law of those States and placed them on the statute books, is enough indeed to cause the Southerner to think it a hopeless chance to get his Slave from them.

---

* I hear it stated that some of these States have abolished this law.

But the *honorable* President says if they would make the effort in good temper. I should like to know if the Constitution says anything about the temper in which the demand is to be made. The President being a *constitutional* man, of course he would not set forth any *doctrine* not *constitutional*.

I will now try the President on the violation of this Fugitive Law. He says that the Fugitive clause is as plainly written as any other clause of the Constitution. Well, then, if so, hostility to that law must be so to the Constitution; and, admitting that to be the fact, he, according to his declaration of constitutional power, has the very same right to force the citizens of those States to strike those unconstitutional laws out of their statute books, as he has to coerce the seceding States back, that had withdrawn on account of its being placed there. Now, let the *honorable* gentleman undertake to force that unconstitutional law off of their statute books, and he will be told that, that is their business, not his. But when the South withdraws herself from these States, on account of the unconstitutionality of these laws, she is called, by the *honorable* President, insurrectionary or revolutionary; consequently, is beneath the notice of the *honorable* President; so much so that an application to that tribunal for recognition would, I suppose, be treated with utter contempt. Such a course is folly to the highest degree, and ignorance to the lowest abyss of unlearned men. But the conception that party takes of the Higher Law will always keep them in darkness.

The reader, perhaps, by this time, may have come to the conclusion that I have somewhat changed my position since writing the first edition, for I pressingly recommended, in that piece, the importance of preserving the Union; and I held on to the same views some time after the election of Mr. Lincoln, hoping that, seeing the confusion his election had caused the country, he and his party would at least modify, or cause to be modified, the hostility to the Fugitive clause. But when I saw every offer made to that party refused and trampled under foot, and when I saw that they were determined to carry out the unconstitutional principles upon which Mr. Lincoln was elected, I could see no other alternative for the Southern States but secession, and form for themselves a Southern Republic.

But I must return to the President and his inaugural. Hear what he says: "I hold that in contemplation of universal law and of the Constitution, the union of these States is perpetual. Perpetuity is implied, if not expressed, in the fundamental law of national Governments. It is safe to assert that no Government proper ever had a provision in its organic law for its own termination. Continue to execute all the express provisions of our national Constitution, and the Union will endure forever "

Well, we will see what this is made of. The President says that he holds that in contemplation of universal law, the Union of these States is perpetual. Well, I hold that his contemplation of universal law is utterly wrong, in that part where he holds to Mr. Seward's Higher Law doctrine, that teaches the birth of all men being free, and that no change can legally be made that will hold good against that contemplation, no matter whether prophetically, miraculously, ecclesiastically, or civilly. As I set this forth in my first edition, I shall pass it by.

The President says, that it is safe to assert that no Government ever had a provision in its own organic Constitution for its termination. That is all very true, but if the people of the Government form it for the protection of their property and themselves, and certain clauses in the Constitution of that Government is violated, the people of one section of the Government being the sole sufferers, while the others are dancing over their misfortunes caused by the very men that were rejoicing over it, it does look to me like the time of its termination had come with the suffering section at least.

But I must pass on, for I have already exceeded my first intention; for I then promised not to meddle with abstract questions. But I have been forced to advert to them in order to make the subject conclusive.

Reader, if you will but take the pains to read the inaugural all through, you will there see the winding course the President has taken to deceive the people of his conservativeness. The President, in the course of his inaugural, in speaking of his intentions, and after saying he considered the Union unbroken, that his intention is to execute the laws in all the United States, unless his rightful masters—the American people—shall withhold the requisite means.

His pretension to conservatism, in this place, is very great indeed, but I doubt the sincerity, for the majority of the American people are against his being President, and have been all the time, but he don't seem to back for that. A majority acquiesce in the decision of the Supreme Court; but I find him speaking of it in

his inaugural with almost contempt.   Let us hear what the Constitution says in regard to this judicial power :

"The judicial power shall extend to all cases in law and equity
arising under this Constitution, the laws of the United States, and
treaties made or which shall be made under their authority; to all
cases affecting ambassadors, other public ministers and consuls;
to all cases of admirality and maratime jurisdiction; to controversies to which the United States shall be a party; to controversies between two or more States: between one State and citizens
of another State: between citizens of different States: between
citizens of the same State, claiming lands under grants of different States, and between a State, as citizens thereof, and foreign
States, citizens or subjects, in all cases affecting ambassadors, other public ministers and consuls, and those in which a State shall
be party, the Supreme Court shall have original jurisdiction.   In
all the other cases before mentioned, the Supreme Court shall have
appellant jurisdiction, both as to law and fact, with such exceptions and under such regulations as the Congress shall make."

This is what the Constitution says in regard to the judicial
power.   Well, then if it gives the Supreme Court the right to settle controversies between States, why do we find the President's
party resisting that settlement?   It was agreed on all hands to
abide by its decision ; but when that infernal party saw that the
Supreme Court could not consistently decide their way, they flew
all to pieces, and said that honorable body was defective.   But
now, they having the power in their own hands, can it be hoped
they will not carry it out according to their own notions and to
Mr. Seward's Higher Law doctrine?   I think not, and if the Slave-
holding States are not justifiable in withdrawing from a section
that had not only declared hostility to their institutions, but had
actually commenced it, by bringing an armed force, with all necessary equipments to carry on a servile war, and placed them at
one of the armories of, and in the very heart of a Slave-holding
State.   But yet we are told by the President that the Southern
States had no constitutional right to secede.   Notwithstanding,
his very party sent them here, letters having been found with
Capt. Brown from some of the leading men of the President's
party.

The President, when presiding over the whole of the United
States had, I think, the appointment of some 30,000 officers in the
Southern States.   These being such men as he now has in his Cab-

inet, diffused all through this country, it would not, it is very likely, taken them longer than one year to have accomplished their
design.

I will now take a broad side view of Mr. Lincoln's whole inaugural, and wind up this addition. He states in the course of his
inaugural, that if the Slave-holder would make an effort in *good
temper*. This, I suppose, implies that if they would go to those
States where the obnoxious laws are enacted, and when they had
advanced within eight or ten feet of the *authorities*, fall on their
knees, and beg them, for God's sake, to please let them have their
fugitives, would be considered in *good temper*.

And, again, in the course of his inaugural, he asks the question,
can a compact formed by the unanimous consent of a majority of
a nation, as people, be broken without a majority of the same? I
will answer his by asking him one. Tell me if the members of
this compact set forth by specified rules, by which each one of the
party were to receive justice, and thereby be benefitted : the object being to extend their peace and prosperity, and secure their
lives and property? I ask if a part should be so ungrateful as to
intrude upon the other's property and rights, directly contrary to
the rule they had all agreed to maintain inviolate, and on demanding a redress, fail to get it, but receive instead an insult, could it
be reasonably expected that the offended party would hold on,
when the offending party had worked corruption to the peace and
property of the offended, and, too, contrary to the letter of the
compact? Would it not be right for the offended party to withdraw, from the fact that the compact had failed to accomplish the
object for which it was formed, consequently was of no more use
to them?

A governmental compact is binding as long as the laws are faith-
fully executed, but no longer.

Again, he says that every member of Congress is sworn to support the whole Constitution, and he says the Fugitive clause is as
plainly written as any clause in the Constitution. But yet we find
him and his party resisting that clause. Now, I do not wish to
say anything that would in any wise invalidate the President's nor
his party's oaths, but it does look strange to me for men who had
taken it, act directly contrary to the purposes for which it was
taken.

I, therefore, hold that the seceding States are perfectly justifiable in seceding ; and I also hold that if they had not done so,

after they had endeavored for a quarter of a century to quell an evil, that they saw was sure to destroy their property, civil privileges, and the religious morals of their children, would have been, I hold, unworthy the name of free men. They, seeing this evil's infernal effects upon their lives and property, what more could they do for their children, than to separate as far as possible from this evil, which had been a hinderance to their onward progress for a quarter of a century; and, instead of it's getting better, was actually getting worse, so much so, that it had actually assumed a formidable position? I hold that had the Slave-holding States, under these inauspicious circumstances, remained in the Union, when every attempt to the claim of an equality in the Union had been contemptuously treated, would have subjected themselves, for a verdict to be given by their rising posterity, against the judgment and patriotism of their forefathers.

Relying on Him who works all things after the counsel of His own will, we look for prosperity and hope for success.